THE GHOST OF DOWN HILL

BY

EDGAR WALLACE

British Library Cataloguing-in-Publication Data
A catalogue record for this book is available from
the British Library

Contents

EDGAR WALLACE

Richard Horatio Edgar Wallace was born in London, England in 1875. He received his early education at St. Peter's School and the Board School, but after a frenetic teens involving a rash engagement and frequently changing employment circumstances, Wallace went into the military. He served in the Royal West Kent Regiment in England and then as part of the Medical Staff Corps stationed in South Africa. However, Wallace disliked army life, finding it too physically testing. Eventually he managed to work his way into the press corps, becoming a war correspondent with the *Daily Mail* in 1898 during the Boer War. It was during this time that Wallace met Rudyard Kipling, a man he greatly admired.

In 1902, Wallace became editor of the *Rand Daily Mail*, earning a handsome salary. However, a dislike of "economising" and a lavish lifestyle saw him constantly in debt. Whilst in the Balkans covering the Russo-Japanese War, Wallace found the inspiration for *The Four Just Men*, published in 1905. This novel is now regarded as the prototype of modern thriller novels. However, by 1908, due to more terrible financial management, Wallace was penniless again, and he and his wife wound up living in a virtual slum in London. A lifeline came in the form of his *Sanders of the River* stories, serialized in a magazine of the day, which (despite being seen to contain pro-imperialist and racist overtones today) were highly popular, and sparked two decades of prolific output from Wallace.

Over the rest of his life, Wallace produced some 173 books and wrote 17 plays. These were largely adventure narratives with elements of crime or mystery, and usually combined a bombastic sensationalism with hammy violence. Arguably his best – and certainly his most successful, sparking as it did a semi-successful stint in Hollywood – work is his 1925 novel *The Gaunt Stranger*, later renamed *The Ringer* for the stage.

Wallace died suddenly in Beverly Hills, California in 1932, aged 57. At the time of his death, he had been earning what would today be considered a multi-million pound salary, yet incredibly, was hugely in debt, with no cash to his name. Sadly, he never got to see his most successful work – the 'gorilla picture' script he had earlier helped pen, which just a year after his death became the 1933 classic, *King Kong*.

THE GHOST
OF DOWN HILL

Edgar Wallace

I

It was, of course, a coincidence that Margot Panton was the guest of Mrs John Staines on the night of the visitation; it was equally a coincidence that she travelled down to Arthurton by the 4.57 in the same railway coupé as Jeremiah Jowlett. And yet it was as natural that she should break her journey in town to accept the hospitality which her old nurse could offer her, as it was that Jeremiah and she should be fellow passengers by the only fast train which Jerry always took, summer and winter, unless he was away from London or was working up evidence against some malefactor; for Jerry was a barrister, and had a desk in the office of the Public Prosecutor.

"My dear," said Martha Staines in genuine admiration, "I should never have known you!"

Margot, a slight, pretty figure curled up in an armchair before the fire, raised her tea cup in warning.

"Don't tell me I'm growing pretty, Martha!" she said solemnly. "Ever since I can remember I have been growing pretty and have never quite grown."

"Well, you've got there now Margot," Martha Staines shook her head and sighed.

The girl's mother had died eight months before, leaving her orphan child in the guardianship of an absent brother-in-law. Martha recalled the sad, thin face of the woman she had served for so many years, and those happy days at Royston when Margot had been the most angelic of babies.

"Your uncle is back, then, Margot?"

The girl nodded, a gleam of amusement in her eyes.

"It is rather fun having a guardian you cannot find!" she said. "I wonder what he will do with me when the travel fever comes on him again?"

Martha shook her head. She was a stout, good-looking woman of forty-five, and her prosperity had neither spoilt her humour nor her manners.

"Where has he been this time?" she asked.

Margot took a letter from her bag and consulted it.

"The Upper Amazon," she said. "I'll read you the letter:

" 'DEAR MARGOT,

" 'I was grieved to learn on my return that my poor sister had passed away. By the letters which I found waiting from your lawyers I see that I am appointed your guardian. I hope you will not find Arthurton a bore. I am rather an old fogey and am interested in very little outside of geology and spiritualism, but you shall be your own mistress. I shall expect you on Tuesday evening.

" 'Your loving uncle,
" 'JAMES STUART.' "

"Spiritualism," said Martha thoughtfully. "That sounds lively."

The girl laughed and put down her cup upon the table. She was at an age when even the supernatural phenomena of life were amusing.

Mr Staines came in a few minutes later. He was a bluff man, red and jovial of face and stout of build. He brought with him a faint fragrance of pine, and the dust of the saw-mill lay like powder on his boots.

"It's a lovely part of the country you're going to, Miss Panton," he said, as he stirred his tea. "I know it very well. What is the name of your uncle?"

"Stuart," said the girl. "Mr James Stuart."

He nodded.

"I know his house, too; a big place at the foot of the hill with a lovely garden – in the proper season. It will be well under snow now."

He scratched his chin.

"Yes, I remember him, a very close gentleman. He had the name of being a little eccentric, if you don't mind my saying so, miss."

"He's a spiritualist, Staines," said Martha.

"A spiritualist, eh?" Mr Staines chuckled.

"Well, he's got plenty of spirits to practise on at Arthurton. Maybe he'll have a go at the Ghost of Down Hill Farm."

"That sounds thrilling," said the girl, wide-eyed. "Do tell me about the Ghost of Down Hill Farm, Mr Staines."

"Well, I've never seen it myself – mother, I'll have another cup of tea – but I've heard yarns about it," said Mr Staines. "In the first place, there isn't a Down Hill Farm. There used to be about eighty years ago, but it's built on now, and before that there was a priory, or a monastery, or something. That is where the ghost comes from. I took the trouble to read up the history years and years ago," he explained almost apologetically. "That is why I know the dates. In 1348 the country, and the continent too, was visited by a terrible plague which took off half the inhabitants of England. It broke out in the Priory, being carried to Arthurton by a monk who came from Yorkshire, and when the villagers heard that they had the plague they put a guard round the place and would allow no one to go in or come out. All the monks died except one, and he used to come out every night and walk round the building. After a time he died too. He is the Ghost of Down Hill – they have dropped

calling it a farm – and I've met old men who say they've
seen him."

"How lovely!" said the girl ecstatically. "Do you think
that he'll walk for me?"

"Well, miss," said Staines with a twinkle in his eye, "if
he wouldn't walk for you, he'd walk for nobody," and his
laugh shook the decanters on the side-board.

Suddenly he became serious and turned to his wife.

"Did I tell you about that case at Eastbourne, mother?"
he asked.

"No, my dear, you didn't," said his wife, busy at the
table clearing up the tea things.

"Did you ever hear me speak about a man named
Wheeler?"

Mrs Staines shook her head.

"Well, I have, lots of times," said Staines. "Anyway, it
doesn't matter. He's in the surveyor's office at Eastbourne
now, but I knew him years ago when he was clerk of the
works for one of the biggest architects in the South of
England. A very nice fellow."

"Well, what about him?" asked Mrs Staines.

"Listen to this."

Mr Staines fumbled in his pocket and produced a pair
of pince-nez which he fixed to his nose, then unfolded the
evening paper, and after a search:

" 'An extraordinary happening is reported from
Eastbourne. Mr Joseph Wheeler, of the Borough
Surveyor's office, was sitting in his room on Sunday
night, the family being at church, when a masked man
appeared and, holding up Mr Wheeler at the point
of a revolver, demanded that he should produce his
bank-books or any other personal accounts he might
have. Fortunately Mr Wheeler had the books handy
and produced them under protest. The intruder then
ordered his victim to stand with his face to the wall
whilst he examined the pass-books which had been
produced. The examination lasted five minutes at the

end of which time the masked man disappeared as suddenly as he came.' "

"Well, now, what do you think of that!" said Mrs Staines, properly impressed.

"I thought it was going to be quite exciting," said the girl, disappointed. "He should at least have left a message written in blood!"

She went to bed early that night. She had had a tiring journey and Mrs Staines, leaving her husband to go to his office to work out the day's accounts, followed her example.

The Staines's house stood at the entrance of one of the timber yards which John Staines, in his affluence, had acquired. A one-story brick building built in the yard formed the headquarters of his thriving business and it was to his own office that he repaired to enter up the personal transactions.

He did not hear the door open but he felt a cold draught of air and looked round. A man was closing the door behind him as he looked and Mr Staines jumped to his feet, for the head of the intruder was enveloped in a monkish cowl and two hard, bright eyes glared at him through the vertical slits which had been cut in the mask. More alarming still was the automatic pistol which he held in his hand.

"Don't shout, and don't attempt to get away. Pull down those blinds," ordered the man; and Staines obeyed, drawing down the blue linen blinds and shutting out all view of the interior from the yard.

"I want your pass-books, bank-books and private ledgers for the past ten years," said the stranger.

"Look here," began Mr Staines.

"Look nowhere," snarled the mask. "Do as you are told, damn you!"

Mr John Staines was a wise man and, albeit resentfully, obeyed. He stacked the little brown covered books on the table, taking them from his safe.

"Now stand against the wall and don't look round," said the intruder and again Mr Staines obeyed.

He heard the rustle of turning leaves but he did not turn his head. Five minutes passed and a chair was pushed back.

"Stand still," said the stranger.

The door opened and closed rapidly, a few seconds later he heard the crash of the wicket gate and sat down heavily in his chair.

"Well, I'm –!" said Mr Staines, and his profanity was pardonable in the circumstances.

II

In a small, gloomy office overlooking Whitehall, Mr Jeremiah Jowlett collected together the dossiers he had been examining, tucked them under his arm and sprinted for the room of his chief. Lord Ilfran looked up as his subordinate came in.

"Hullo, Jerry, haven't you gone?" he asked.

"No, sir," said Jerry unnecessarily, and put the envelopes before the elder man. "I think we can prosecute in the cases of Myer and Burton," he said, "but there does not seem to be a case against Townsend."

Lord Ilfran nodded.

"Is there any fresh news?" he asked.

"None sir, of any importance. I see in the newspapers that an attempt has been made to rob the strong rooms of the mail steamer *Carmuria* but the thieves seem to have bungled it very badly, and the men are in custody at Southampton."

"There are no good strong-room robbers left," said Lord Ilfran in a tone which suggested that he regretted the circumstances. "Ever since the Flack gang were laid by the heels that branch of crime has become uninteresting. What is this I see," he asked, "about the hold-up of a wood merchant in Camberwell?"

"Oh, yes," Jerry was leaving but turned back. "That is extraordinary. There was a man held up in similar circumstances at Eastbourne two or three days ago and now this man Staines has been victimized."

"Nothing was stolen?" asked Lord Ilfran.

"Nothing at all, apparently," replied Jerry. "As in the previous case, the burglar merely asked to see the state of the pass-books and the private ledgers of Mr Staines."

"Extraordinary!" murmured Lord Ilfran looking out of the window. "Most extraordinary! Nothing was stolen you say?"

"Nothing at all," said Jerry and threw a glance at the clock above the head of the Public Prosecutor.

"Well, get off," said Ilfran with a smile. "I suppose you are catching your 4.57. What on earth makes you live at Arthurton?"

"Come down and spend Christmas with me, sir," said Jerry with a smile, "and I think you'll understand."

The taxi-cab that took him to Victoria was a slow one and he had to race to the platform and even then only arrived as the train was on the move. The guard opened the door of a first-class carriage and he jumped in and would have fallen but a little hand thrust out in alarm saved him.

"I am so awfully sorry," said Jerry with that smile of his which had disarmed so many of his critics.

"I think the train jerked," said Margot Panton primly.

"I'm almost sure it jerked," said Jeremiah, and then he chuckled and the girl laughed too.

It was all very improper, of course, and very unusual. Margot had been warned since she could understand never to speak to strange men in railway carriages, and never under any circumstances to travel alone with one. And yet before the train had reached Clapham Junction Jerry had told her that his favourite name for aunts was Maud and she had explained the inner workings of the prefect system at the school she had left.

"Arthurton!" he said in delight when she told him her

destination. "Good lord, I'm going there, too. Where are you staying?"

"With my guardian, Mr James Stuart."

"Is that so?" he said, raising his eyebrows. "Why, we're neighbours! Mr Stuart is the antiquarian or explorer, or something, isn't he? I know he lives abroad."

"I know very little about him," she replied, "and I don't remember having seen him. He is the only relative I have in the world," she said simply.

Jerry was more than ordinarily interested and plied her with questions as to her length of stay until laughingly she changed the subject.

"If you live at Arthurton –"

"As I swear I do," he said.

"Don't interrupt. If you live at Arthurton you can tell me something I'm dying to hear about."

"I have a bronze medal for saving life," he said modestly. "I must tell you this in case nobody else does. I am willing to earn another one."

"Have you ever seen the Ghost of Down Hill?" she asked.

He fell back in his seat and shrieked with laughter.

"I am the Ghost of Down Hill," he said, and she stared at him. "At least I'm the only ghost that's ever haunted Down Hill. My house is built, if not upon the site, at least upon the land which the old monks owned and which the proprietor of Down Hill Farm, which was burnt a hundred years ago, included in his demesne."

"And you've never seen the ghost?" she asked.

"I've never seen the ghost, and Minter – he is my valet, cook and general manager – hasn't seen a ghost either."

He hesitated and then:

"No, we've seen nothing."

"You were going to say 'except,' " she began.

He smiled.

"Except that two or three nights ago we saw a strange figure in the garden, but it was probably a poacher setting a snare. There are thousands of rabbits on that part of the Downs.

"You'll love the place," he said as he helped her to alight at Treen Station, "and I hope your uncle is going to invite me to tea and tennis. You've got a wonderful court and I have no court at all. And there is your uncle. Shall I introduce you?" he asked whimsically.

The man who walked towards her was a little above middle height and strongly built. Apparently he was in the region of sixty but he was as straight as a ramrod. The short-clipped white beard, the shaggy eyebrows and the large nose gave her the impression of an old eagle; an impression which the bright deep-set eyes helped to strengthen. He gave her smile for smile as he met her and took her little hand in his big, hairy paw. Though it was bitterly cold and the snow lay thick on the roads, he wore no overcoat nor gloves and the soft white shirt was open at the neck to expose the corded throat.

"You're Margot," he said, and brushed her cheek with his lips. "How do you do, Mr Jowlett. This is a neighbour of ours, Margot."

His manner was brusque, his voice gruff but his attitude was genial. He had a little car waiting at the station yard. It was parked alongside Jerry's one extravagance, a long-bonneted racing car, the possession of which he excused on account of its hill-climbing qualities.

"It is my elevator," he said. "I live on the first floor of the world, Miss Panton, a position which gives me the happy feeling of being able to look down upon my fellow-citizens."

They gave him a minute's start and he disappeared silently across the snowy carpet.

James Stuart sat at the wheel and his little car followed at a respectable distance. He did not speak to the girl and she had time to take stock of this new relative who had come into her life. He had the glamour of relationship to her mother, but she felt that she could love this grim old man, upon whose face she thought she detected the lines of suffering.

Mr Staines had not exaggerated the prettiness of her new home. It was an old house, creeper-grown, and stood in extensive grounds. Even under its white, fleecy covering, which lay in thick pads on the spreading cedars, she saw the beautiful possibilities of the sleeping garden.

"I wonder you can ever leave this place," she said as she stood looking through the french windows of the drawing-room.

"It's pretty," he said shortly.

"Is there anything in Brazil as pretty?"

He shook his head.

"Nothing," he answered shortly.

Her own apartment was a lovely large room overlooking the garden and had the appearance of having been recently furnished. She discovered later that this was the fact and that the furniture had only arrived that day from Eastbourne.

She found her uncle amiable enough at dinner. He had a fund of sardonic humour which kept her amused and he took, moreover, a surprisingly broad view of men and things.

"There isn't much young company for you in Arthurton," he said. "A girl like you should have plenty of dances and similar nonsense. I'll invite young Jowlett over to dinner to-morrow night if you like."

She did like very much.

"In the season there's plenty of social life in Eastbourne, and it is only fourteen miles away, and I'm thinking of getting another car," he said. "But now –" he hesitated and rubbed his beard with his knuckles, a little gesture of irritation which did not escape her – "I am very busy in the evenings with my specimens and I'm afraid you'll be left alone –"

"Please don't worry about me, Uncle James," she said earnestly. "I can amuse myself with a book. And if I think I'm on your mind all the time, it will take half the fun out of life."

He seemed relieved at this, and then awkwardly:

"Well, you can start right away," he said. "I am going to my study now."

At ten o'clock she tapped at his door to say good-night and went up to her room. He had promised her a maid, though she was ready enough to dispense with this luxury. She undressed and sat in her kimono by the open window looking over the garden. It was the third quarter of the moon and it was rising as she looked out upon that most wonderful of landscapes.

The snowy expanse of the Downs lay in blue shadow and the moonlight flooded the broad white Weald with an uncanny radiance.

She sighed happily, switched off the light and snuggled into bed. The strangeness of the room and, perhaps, the queer smell which all new furniture has, prevented her sleeping as soundly as she expected. She turned from side to side, dozing fitfully, and then she heard the faint sound of a foot on the gravel path outside. From the position of the patch of moon-light on the floor she knew it must be very late and wondered if her uncle was in the habit of taking midnight strolls on such a freezing night. Slipping out of bed she pulled on her dressing-gown, walked to the window, and looked out.

And then her blood froze, and her knees gave under her, for there in the middle of the garden path, standing out against the snowy background, was a figure in the sombre habit of a monk!

The cowl was drawn over his head and the face was invisible.

It stood there motionless, its hands concealed in its wide sleeves, its head bent as in thought. Then slowly the head turned and the moonlight fell upon the bony face, the hollow sockets of its eyes, the white gleam of its fleshless teeth.

For a moment she stared, paralysed, incapable of sound or movement; and then she found her voice, and with a shrill scream collapsed on the floor in a dead faint.

III

·When she came to herself she was lying on the bed under the eider-down quilt and her uncle's anxious face was looking down at hers. He was in his dressing-gown and his hair was rumpled untidily.

"I am such a fool," she said, with an apologetic smile.

"I heard you scream. What was the matter – nightmare?" asked Mr Stuart.

And then she told him what she had seen. Stuart walked to the window and looked out.

"A manifestation," he said gravely. "You were very fortunate."

"A manifestation?" she repeated in amazement. "Do you believe –"

He shrugged his shoulders.

"I believe there is a great deal one doesn't understand; a great many things and a great many phenomena," he replied. "But honestly, I think in this case you have been suffering from nightmare."

"Do you – do you think," she faltered, "that was the Ghost of Down Hill?"

She heard him chuckle.

"So you've heard the yarn, have you?" he said. "Perhaps it was. Perhaps it was oyster patty followed by coffee – a combination which has produced more ghosts than any of us spiritualists have raised."

Margot Panton was neither superstitious nor a sceptic. She had the *mens sana in corpore sano* of the well-balanced public school girl, and she was heartily ashamed of the exhibition she had made of herself. It had been the surprise of it; the atmosphere of mystery; the moonlight; the strangeness of the place – all these circumstances had combined to surprise her into that ridiculous fainting fit.

Alone in her room, she sat up in bed clasping her knees, a picture of frowning puzzlement. Her common-sense told her that there was no such thing as ghosts and they did not wear boots that crunched the gravel beneath them. She got out of bed again and looked out into the garden. It was empty. Then switching off the light with a contemptuous "pooh!" she curled herself in bed and fell into a dreamless sleep.

Her uncle was out when she came down to breakfast but he returned before she had finished the meal.

"Well, have you got over your scare?" he asked as he dropped his hand on her shoulder in passing her.

"I'm perfectly certain it wasn't a ghost," she said.

"Oh, you are, are you?" his eyes twinkled, "and how do you reach that conclusion?"

"Ghosts don't wear boots," she said decidedly.

"They may have shoes," said the dry old man. "I take tea without sugar or milk, Margot. If it was not a ghost, then I ought to be very careful," he said. "I have brought some rather valuable things back from Brazil and Peru; some old statuettes of the Incas," he explained, but did not offer to show them to her.

She had had a glimpse of his study that morning, a plainly furnished room on the ground floor with a book-case and a desk, a few skins of animals stretched on the walls and little else.

That morning she was still occupied in unpacking her trunk and disposing of her photographs about the room.

She lunched alone, her uncle having gone to Hastings in his car. When he had told her he was making this trip she had expected he would invite her and he must have guessed her thoughts.

"When I get a better car I'll take you round the country, Margot, but you make my old flivver look shabby."

She smiled at the implied compliment. She was beginning to like this old man with his mordant humour and his pretty turn of compliment.

His absence gave her an opportunity of exploring her new domain, and putting on a pair of heavy boots – for the snow lay thick upon the hillside, under a radiant sun – she went out on a tour of inspection. Beyond the garden was a wide paddock which ran up the hill and was divided from the next property by a wire fence. She followed this fence to the crest of the rise and saw that it passed close to a pretty little brick bungalow which stood on the top of the hill. This must be Down Hill she thought. It covered a larger area than she had imagined. She caught a glimpse of bachelor comfort through the wide open windows. A stout man, whom she rightly guessed was Jeremiah Jowlett's factotum, gave her a stiff little bow as she came abreast of him. He was shovelling away the snow that had fallen in the night from the garden path. Apparently Jerry had gone to town.

"Good morning, madam," he said respectfully.

"Good morning," she replied, smiling, and walked on in silence.

All around, the snow sparkled in the sunlight. Suddenly she was aware of a figure coming towards her. It took her only a glance to see the man was a tramp.

As he drew closer, Margot felt a twinge of unease. Putting her hand in her pocket she chanced upon a shilling and decided to give it to the man. She handed it to him without a word.

"Thank you kindly. Mind you, I'm a rich man by rights, if every man had his due."

He volunteered the information and paused at the end as though he expected her to make some reply. She quickened her pace but recognized the futility, and even danger, of running from a danger which was probably non-existent, and when they came again in sight of the house and the placid servant leaning on his shovel, she recovered something of her lost self-possession.

"There's a ghost around here, so they tell me," said the tramp, and she looked at him more carefully.

He was a hollow-faced man with small eyes set close together and a long aggressive nose. She thought his age was something between forty and fifty.

"I shall be round here for a day or two," he said. "My name's Sibby Carter. I'll just be hanging around."

In spite of herself she laughed.

"I don't know why you should tell me that," she said. "I am really not interested in your plans."

"Sibby Carter my name is," he repeated, and smacked his lips, "and I shall be hanging around here for two or three days."

She was walking away from him when he followed and caught her arm with a grip that made her wince.

"Here, I can tell you something," he began but the stout servant had seen, and with a surprising agility had leapt the hedge and was coming towards them.

"Clear out of here. What do you mean by accosting this lady?"

Sibby Carter released his hold and his thin lips curled up in a sneer that showed his yellow teeth.

"Hello, fat and ugly!" he said rudely. "What are you coming interfering with me for?"

The girl, breathless and a little white, had instinctively drawn to the stout man's side.

"You be off," said Mr Jowlett's servant peremptorily.

"I've as much right here as you have," said Sibby Carter.

"You're on private property, you know that! Now be off, or I'll take you down to the village and give you in charge."

The tramp seemed impressed at this possibility and he looked from the girl to the stout man, and then:

"Fat and ugly!" he shouted. "Fat and ugly!" and went trudging back the way he had come, his shoulders hunched, his hands in his pockets.

IV

When James Stuart returned the girl told him of her unpleasant experience and he listened with a grave face.

"As a rule we see few tramps in this neighbourhood," he said. "You must not go out alone, Margot. What did he call himself?"

"Sibby Carter!" she repeated with a half smile, but Mr Stuart did not smile.

"I must remember that name. It may be useful for purposes of identifying him," he said. "We must thank Mr Jowlett for the service that his servant has rendered us."

He himself met Jeremiah at the station that night, and Jeremiah, whose work had suffered that day by the memory of two laughing grey eyes, accepted the invitation to dine with indecent haste.

"I am glad Minter was on hand," he said. "Confound that fellow! But that was Minter all over. Ever the knight-errant and rescuer of distressed ladies – lucky devil! Do you dress at nights?"

"No, no," said Mr Stuart, shaking his head. "I want you to come as you are. Perhaps you'll drive straight to the house."

"I'll take the elevator to the ninth," said Jeremiah, "and I'll be back at the house in time to welcome you."

But when he did get to Arthurton Lodge Mr Stuart was waiting. The dinner was a great success from the point of view of two people who rallied one another as though they had been friends since childhood. The old man was a silent but appreciative audience.

"And so you actually saw the ghost! And he wore hob-nailed boots. Bully for the ghost," he said boisterously.

"It's fun for you but I was scared to death," said the girl.

"You were afraid I'd lose him I suppose," said Jerry, "and thank you for your thoughtfulness. He certainly had no right to stray on to your property, and any time you see him away from his ancestral home I hope you will send him back. I must get some slippers for him," he said gravely. "You have no idea how that ghost wears out boots –"

"You haven't seen him yet!" she challenged. "You won't speak so flippantly of him when you do."

"I never speak flippantly of ghosts," protested Jerry. "Certainly not of my own ghost. When I bought the property five years ago and built that bungalow I particularly asked for special provision to be made for William –"

"Who is William?" asked the unsuspecting girl.

"William is the name of the ghost," said the other solemnly.

"You're incorrigible. And besides you know uncle takes quite a different view."

"About ghosts?" asked the other incredulously.

"Don't you uncle?" the girl appealed. Mr Stuart rubbed his beard.

"Naturally I believe in manifestations," he said. "I have witnessed some extraordinary psychic phenomena and I would not exclude the possibility of even a ghost."

"I'm sorry if I –" began Jerry.

"You can say anything you like about them," said the old man good-humouredly. "I'm merely expressing an opinion."

They adjourned to the drawing-room after dinner and to the girl's surprise Mr Stuart accompanied them and sat whilst she sang. It was in an interval of silence, one of those momentary cessations of speech which the superstitious associate with the twentieth minute, that an interruption came. The girl looked round suddenly at the shuttered window.

"What was that?" asked Mr Stuart quickly.

"I thought I heard a sound," she said. "It was as though somebody had touched the window pane."

Jerry rose.

"I'll go and see," he said, but the hand of James Stuart detained him.

"It may be our friend the ghost," he said, half jocularly and half seriously, "and in that case I think that somebody should see him who takes a less frivolous view."

"Shall I come with you?" asked Jerry.

"I'd rather go alone," replied Mr Stuart, and was gone for some time.

They heard his footsteps walking along the gravel path which ran round the house and then they heard him return.

It was some minutes before he came back to them and he met Jerry in the passage.

"Miss Panton was getting anxious," said the young man.

"Nobody was there," explained Stuart as he came back to the drawing-room and laid an electric torch upon a table. "I searched the shrubbery and the garden but there is no sign of ghost or burglar."

"It may have been the creeper knocking against the window," said Margot, but Stuart shook his head.

"There is no wind and I particularly noticed that the creeper is trimmed close near the window," he said. "Perhaps it was your imagination."

They sat talking for some time and the old man included himself in the conversation. Jerry was hoping that the scientist would tell something of his adventures in Brazil but beyond a perfunctory and superficial reference to the heat and the mosquitoes he said little or nothing and the talk was mostly of Margot's school life and Mr Stuart's reminiscences of her mother when she was a girl.

He was in the midst of one of these stories when he stopped suddenly and bent his head.

"Did you hear anything?" he asked.

"I heard nothing," said Jerry in surprise. "What did it sound like?"

"It sounded like a footstep on the gravel. Did you hear it Margot?"

But Margot had not heard it either.

"Strange!" muttered Mr Stuart.

The conversation was resumed. Again he stopped.

"I'll swear I heard a cry," he said.

Jerry had heard what he thought was the faint screech of a distant owl.

"I thought it was an owl, too," said Margot.

Soon after Jerry rose to go and they walked with him to the hall, Mr Stuart helping him on with his coat. He had left his car at the back of the house outside the little garage but refused the old man's company.

"I can find my way up the hill road blind-folded," he said as Stuart opened the door, "and –"

He stopped and started back with a little exclamation of surprise. And well he might be surprised, for crouched in the porch was the figure of a man. The light in the hall was strong enough to show every detail of the huddled man and Margot recognized him.

"Why, it is the tramp!" she cried. "Sibby Carter."

Jerry leant over the figure and touched it, and at that touch it rolled over and fell in an inanimate heap.

"Dead!" gasped Jerry and looked closer.

As the figure lay its throat was exposed and there was a round and livid bruise at the nape of the neck.

"Dead!" said Jerry again. "And murdered I think. The Ghost of Down Hill has a pair of very powerful hands, Mr Stuart, for this man's neck is broken!"

V

There was no doubt about it. The man was dead. Jeremiah had only to look at him for a second to see that. Gently he shepherded the girl back to the drawing-room. She was white but very calm, and when she spoke her voice did not so much as tremble.

"Is he dead?" she asked quietly, and marvelling at her self-possession, Jeremiah nodded.

"How dreadful! What do you think happened?"

"My mind is in a whirl," said Jeremiah, shaking his head helplessly. "I know no more than you."

"I am sure he is the man whose name was Sibby Carter," she said, and he looked at her in astonishment, for he had not heard her half-whispered words when the body had been found.

"Do you know him?" he asked incredulously.

She shook her head.

"I only met him to-day," she said, and she told him again of her meeting with the tramp.

"That man?" he said in surprise; "what an extraordinary coincidence!"

It was an hour before the police came, and nearly two hours before the ambulance arrived from Eastbourne to carry away the victim of the tragedy.

The fact that Jeremiah had been present in the house relieved Mr Stuart from the cross-examination of the detective-officer, who came in haste with the ambulance.

"It was very fortunate you were here," said James Stuart gravely. "I can't understand it. Why did the man come here, and who but the Ghost of Down Hill could have slain him?"

In other circumstances Jeremiah would have laughed.

"The Ghost of Down Hill?" he repeated; "but surely, Mr Stuart, a ghost is not a material thing with material strength in its substantial fingers?"

James Stuart shook his head.

"There are more things in this world than are dreamt of in your philosophy," he said simply, and with these words in his ears Jeremiah made his way back to his bungalow, a greatly perturbed man.

Although the hour was late, the stout and placid Minter was waiting for him; a little fire burnt in the grate of his comfortable sitting room, and Minter, who never seemed to be tired, listened to the story of the "exciting night" with that air of polite interest which invariably annoyed Jeremiah.

He was a large, stout, calm man with a clean-shaven face and deep-set eyes, the very model of a perfect valet-butler, but there were times when he irritated Jeremiah beyond endurance. The man had been in his service for five months, and in every way had been satisfactory, and now Jeremiah had a particular reason for being grateful to him. He had that morning saved the girl from the unpleasant attentions of the dead Sibby Carter.

"One would imagine, Minter," he said irritably, "that I was telling you the story of a tea-fight. Don't you realize that there has been a murder committed under your very nose?"

"Oh yes, sir," said Minter respectfully. "What time would you like your breakfast in the morning?"

"Pah!" said Jeremiah.

He dismissed his servant, and went to bed. But his mind was too active to sleep. Again and again he turned over in his mind the extraordinary circumstances of that evening, and somehow the adventure of the surveyor of Eastbourne, and Mr Staine's curious experience, insisted upon obtruding into his mind and mixing themselves up until, with a groan, he shut his eyes tight and attempted to dismiss entirely from his thoughts both the Ghost of Down Hill and the mystery man who held up inoffensive people and examined their pass-books.

He was nearly asleep when he thought he heard a stealthy movement outside his door, and was instantly awake. He listened. Again it came, a faint creak of sound, and carefully pulling back the clothes, he got out of bed as noiselessly as possible, crept to the door and listened.

The clock of Arthurton church struck three.

"This is getting on my nerves," he muttered to himself and would have gone back to bed, but for the unexpected repetition of the sound. This time it was outside the house. He walked across the room to the window and gently drew aside the curtain. The cloud wrack had for a moment covered the moon, but he could see a figure walking quickly down the snow-covered path to the gate, and there was no mistaking its identity, for the bulk of the man could not be disguised. It was Minter!

He pulled on his trousers over his pyjamas, slipped his feet into long mosquito boots, and bundling on an overcoat, he went out into the passage through the door which was open, along the covered passage way, and out of the side door, which also was ajar.

When he got outside the man had reached the gate.

"Minter," he called sharply, and at the sound of his voice Minter turned. He was carrying something in his hand; something that glittered and gleamed in a fitful ray of moonlight.

"Minter," called Jeremiah again.

"Yes, sir," was the answer, and the man came slowly back.

Before he could slip the thing he carried into his pocket, Jeremiah had seen the revolver, and gasped. He did not link the mild Minter with lethal weapons.

"What the devil are you doing crawling about in the middle of the night with a pistol in your hand," he demanded.

"I was following the Ghost of Down Hill, sir," was the cool reply.

"The Ghost of Down Hill," repeated Jeremiah, "what do you mean?"

Minter did not reply immediately, and Jeremiah, scrutinizing him keenly, saw that he was considerably perturbed by the unexpected interruption to his quest.

"I thought I saw a figure moving through the gardens here and I followed it."

Jeremiah looked at him.

"But you're fully dressed, Minter," he said quietly. "Did you happen to be fully dressed when you saw the ghost?"

"Yes, sir," was the surprising reply.

Jeremiah led the way back to the sitting room and turned on the light, and this time his examination of his servant was more thorough.

"And did you happen to have changed your clothes before you went to bed," he asked pointedly, for the suit the man wore was not the butler's uniform that had encased his portly figure when Jeremiah had said good-night to him.

Minter did not make any reply.

"I will see you about this in the morning," said Jeremiah, and with a curt nod dismissed his servant.

The more he thought the matter over, the more puzzled he became. A faint glow was showing in the east before he eventually fell into a troubled sleep, to be awakened by the correct Minter, who came into the room with a preliminary knock, carrying the usual morning tea-service.

The man filled Jeremiah's bath and put his clothes ready before he spoke.

"I daresay, sir," he said, after a moment's hesitation, "that you think my conduct last night was rather strange."

"I think it was extremely strange," said Jeremiah, "and I tell you this frankly, Minter, that unless you explain what you were doing out in the middle of the night, and explain it to my satisfaction, I shall dispense with your services."

Minter's heavy head nodded.

"That I can quite understand, sir," he said politely, "but if I tell you, sir, that I have seen the Ghost of Down Hill three nights in succession, and that I was waiting last night to follow him, you will understand that there is nothing mysterious about my having changed my clothes for garments more suitable for an out-of-door chase.

This argument was unanswerable. Jeremiah did not for one moment doubt the big man's word. He also had seen the Ghost of Down Hill, and it was quite possible that the man was speaking the truth.

"Ghosts, sir," the man went on, "do not as a rule impress me because I come from a long line of Wesleyan Methodists who are not great believers in spiritual manifestations. But a ghost with a theodolite and a measures-rod seems to me to be a little outside of the usual run of ghosts."

"What do you mean Minter?" asked Jeremiah quickly, as he sat on the edge of the bed staring at the man.

"Two nights ago, sir, I saw the ghost, and he carried over his shoulder a small theodolite – I saw it in use later. He was making elaborate measurements, evidently starting from the big rock in the sunken garden below the house, for I saw the rod as distinctly as I see you. Before I could dress and get out he was gone."

Jeremiah whistled. All doubt as to his servant's story was now dissipated. He knew that the man was speaking the truth.

"You must have found his footprints?"

"I found them immediately after, sir, but was unable to make a very careful observation in the morning because another fall of snow fell during the night," said Minter, shaking his head, and Jeremiah had to laugh at the matter-of-fact tone of his servitor.

"Aren't you a bit scared, Minter?"

"No, sir, I'm not very scared," said the man with a smile. "Not so scared as the ghost would be if he knew that I took the revolver prize at Bisley for three years in succession."

VI

"It is an extraordinary case," said Lord Ilfran shaking his head. "One of the most extraordinary I have ever heard about."

He was seated at his desk in the big room overlooking Whitehall and Jeremiah Jowlett was sitting on the opposite side of the table facing him.

Lord Ilfran ran his long, nervous fingers through his white hair, and stared out of the window.

"You say that this man Carter was a member of the Flack gang."

Jeremiah nodded.

"I don't think there can be any doubt about that," he said. "His finger-prints have been taken and identified; moreover, he didn't seem to disguise his name. He went to prison at the same time as John Flack, the head of the gang, and they were released from prison within a few days of one another."

"Has Flack been discovered?"

"No, sir," replied Jeremiah. "We have put a call out to all stations, but up to now we have not been able to pull him in."

"It's curious," said the Public Prosecutor again, "and what a terrible shock for that poor girl."

"She stood it splendidly," said the enthusiastic Jeremiah. "Most women would have fainted, but she was a brick."

"There were no footsteps in the snow?"

"No. The garden path had been swept clear of snow, and

the only clue we have is the one supplied by Mr Stuart. He said he thought he heard footsteps a few minutes before the tragedy was discovered."

Lord Ilfran leant back in his chair.

"The ghost suggestion is, of course, absurd," he said. "Somebody is masquerading for a purpose of his own. By-the-way, have you seen the ghost?"

"Twice," said Jeremiah to his chief's surprise. "The fact is sir –" he leant across the table and lowered his voice – "so far as a house can be said to be haunted, that description applies to my bungalow. I haven't told Miss Panton because I didn't want to alarm her, but the Ghost of Down Hill is a very real quantity, and although my glimpses of this midnight wanderer have been more or less sketchy, yet the descriptions Miss Panton gave me of the man in the monk's robe with a grinning skeleton face are identical with what I saw."

Lord Ilfran was seldom surprised. A lifetime spent in the law had removed the novelty even from the bizarre, but now he was genuinely amazed, for Jeremiah was a hard-headed young man, who had few illusions.

"How long has this been going on?" he asked curiously.

"About six months," was the reply, "or about three months before Mr Stuart returned from the Brazils. The first time I saw the 'ghost' was one late summer night when a storm was working up from the sea. I was sitting in my study reading a law book, when I heard a tap-tap at the window. I thought that a shutter had worked loose and took no notice. Presently it was repeated. I walked to the window and looked out; it was a pitch black night and I saw nothing until suddenly there came a blinding flash of lightning, and there, standing in the middle of the path, I saw the figure of a monk. By the time I had got outside it was raining heavily, and the fitful flashes of lightning failed to reveal the visitor.

"The second time was a month ago, and on this occasion the visitation was a little more serious," said Jeremiah quietly. "I had gone to bed and was asleep when Minter woke me to tell me he heard a noise in the cellar. We have a cellar beneath the house where I keep a small stock of wine. When I went to investigate I discovered the cellar door wide open, and on going down I found that somebody had dug a deep hole in the floor of the cellar."

"You saw nobody?" asked Lord Ilfran intensely interested.

"Nobody," replied Jeremiah, "at the moment. Behind the house is a covered passage-way which communicates with the kitchen, and affords me storage for my bicycle and a side entrance to the garage. In my search of the house I reached the passage-way, carrying a petrol lantern, and then I saw the visitor for the second time He was at the far end of the passage near the side door, and I am willing to confess that the sight of that fleshless face startled me. Before I could reach him he was gone."

"Has there been any other manifestation?"

Jeremiah smiled.

'It is curious you should use that word, sir," he said, still smiling. "It is a favourite one of Mr James Stuart, who implicitly believes in spirits, and has asked me to give him permission to spend a night alone in the house in order that he may lay the ghost. I might add," he went on, "that Minter, my servant, has also seen the figure – a fact which I learnt only last night."

Lord Ilfran rose from his table and paced the room slowly.

"That will not bring us any nearer to the discovery of the murderer of Sibby Carter," he said. "Are you going to fall in with Mr Stuart's suggestion?"

"I don't know why I shouldn't," said Jeremiah. He did not explain that he was particularly anxious to be on good terms with the uncle of Margot Panton, and that as Mr Stuart had offered him the use of his own house during the period of his ghost laying, he was all the more willing and ready to humour the old man in his whim.

"Yes. sir." he said. "I am taking Minter down to Mr Stuart's house the day after to-morrow."

"That is Christmas Eve," interrupted Lord Ilfran, "and a very excellent time for ghosts. I am sure I wish Mr Stuart luck."

Jeremiah Jowlett went home that night a little earlier. He was anxious to see the girl who had made so profound an impression upon him, and more anxious to earn whether any new evidence had come to light. He found Margot amazingly cheerful. Perhaps it had been her first shock which had steeled her to the subsequent tragedy, but at any rate, she was less distressed than he had dared to expect.

"Uncle is out," she said. "Will you have some tea with me?"

Jeremiah did not want a second invitation. He lingered over the repast till it was nearly dinner time, but Mr James Stuart had not returned, and at last he reluctantly took his leave.

It was a beautiful night, despite the cold, and they stood for a moment talking at the garden gate. From where they were the outlines of Down Hill house stood clear against the dying light in the western sky.

"I have allowed Minter to go home to see his sister," explained Jeremiah, when the girl had remarked upon the darkness of the bungalow. "Please don't worry about me, Miss Panton; I am an accomplished bachelor, who can grill a chop and boil a potato, with the best cook in Arthurton."

"It seems horribly lonely for you," said Margot. "Won't you stay to dinner?"

"I'd like to," said Jeremiah in all sincerity, "but I don't want to annoy your uncle by living on the premises."

Suddenly she clutched his arm.

"Look!" she gasped, and pointed to the house.

He could only stare in speechless amazement.

Of a sudden every window in the little building was glowing redly, as though simultaneously every room was on fire. Fiercely it gleamed across the snow-white hill, and then as suddenly the red glow died down.

"I must investigate this," said Jeremiah.

"Let me come with you," she said, and he felt her grip tighten on his arm, and hesitated.

"I think you had better stay here," he said, and a minute later she heard the thunder of his car as it took the steep hill road.

Jerry jumped from the machine at the entrance to his demesne, and raced along the garden path. Switching on a pocket lamp he tried the side door. It was locked. He thrust a key into the lock and a second later was in the covered passage. He did not meet any intruder, nor did he expect to. There was a strong smell of sulphur and the dining room, the first he entered, was hazy with smoke. A small fire, which Minter had lit before he went out, glowed on the hearth; but the room was empty, as was his bedroom, where another small fire was burning.

He searched every inch of the bungalow without finding the slightest trace of a visitor. It was impossible that anybody could have made their escape, for all the doors, except the side door, were locked on the inside, and the side door had a lock which he had recently put on, which he knew it was impossible to pick.

He came back to the dining-room, and then, for the first time, saw a document which lay upon the table. It was not of paper, but of old-fashioned vellum, and the words were written in quaint old English characters:

"Thy presence on this hallowed spot is a profanation. Leave thy house, lest the lonely monk of Down Hill bring thee to a terrible death."

VII

How had the paper got there? He looked round and the solution became apparent. The table was placed near to the window, and above the window were two small ventilating panes, one of which was open. The paper could have been thrust in from the outside and the chances were that it would fall upon the table. He opened the window to let the fumes disperse and then sat down to puzzle out the situation.

Suddenly a thought struck him, and he went to the fire and looked at it carefully. On the top of the red glowing coal were the ashes of paper. He went into the next room and made a similar discovery. Slowly a smile dawned on his face.

"So that's it, is it?" he muttered and went out of the house taking with him a step ladder which stood in the passage. His home was built into the hill rather than upon it, and the fields behind were almost on a level with the roof. He planted his step ladder and climbed carefully. In a second he was standing on a small stone parapet which surrounded the roof. There was no doubt now as to what the visitor had done; the snow-covered slates were marked in all directions with footprints, and they led up to the squat chimney stack. He made an inspection and returned to his room. Whoever the Ghost of Down Hill was, there was no doubt as to the method he had employed for producing the effect which had so startled Jeremiah and the girl. Two packages of red fire had been dropped down the two chimneys simultaneously, had fallen into the fire, and had ignited, producing that red glow.

He went back to where he had left his car and drove down the hill again to reassure the girl whom he found waiting wrapped in her furs at the garden gate of Mr Stuart's house.

"Nothing very startling," he said carelessly. "Some fireworks that I had intended using to celebrate the coming of the New Year had been left too close to the fire, and were touched off."

"It might have been serious," said the girl. "Your house might have been burnt down."

"I don't think it was as bad as that," said Jeremiah.

He stood talking to the girl for some time, and then

went back to the house. Half-way up the hill he thought he saw a figure crouching in the shelter of some bushes, and stopping the car with a jerk, jumped out. The man turned to run, but Jeremiah was on him before he had gone a few paces.

"Let me have a look at you, my friend," he said as he gripped the stranger's arm; and then he fell back in surprise, for the man was Minter.

"What the dickens do you mean by sneaking away into the bushes?" demanded the exasperated Jerry. "Now see here, Minter, I have had just as much of this mystery as I am willing to stand. You will come up to the house and explain what you are doing here when you are supposed to be in London attending the sick bed of your sister."

The man made no reply, but stepping on to the running-board of the car as it moved, accompanied Jerry back to the house.

"Now, Minter," said Jeremiah grimly, as he closed the door. "I won't trouble you to spin a yarn about the Ghost of Down Hill; I will even excuse you the lie that you were returning home, and that you mistook me for the monkish bogey and hid from fear. Let us have the truth."

Minter was dressed in a rough knicker-bocker suit, over which he wore a heavy Irish ulster. He did not seem in the least embarrassed by his employer's direct questions, and his placid face remained impassive all the time Jerry was talking.

"I have no explanation to give, sir," he said in a smooth, even way, "if you will not accept the story that I was returning to the house when you overtook me."

"Why did you run away?" asked Jeremiah sternly.

"That, I admit, was an error," replied Minter, gravely inclining his head. "I should have stood my ground and offered my explanation. The truth is, Mr Jowlett, I did not think that the occupant of the car was you."

"Nonsense," snapped Jerry, "you know the sound of my car as well as you know the sound of Big Ben. Now, what have you to say for yourself?"

But Minter had evidently no explanation to offer, for he remained silent.

"Very good," said Jeremiah, "then you leave my service to-morrow, you understand, Minter? I will not have these infernal mysteries."

Suddenly a thought struck him.

"You haven't by chance been perambulating the roof of the bungalow to-night?" he asked sardonically, and Minter smiled.

"No, sir, I did not go on to the roof," he said, "but I have been wandering about the house; it is possible you may have observed my footmarks, though I was careful to keep to the paths as much as possible."

"Did you see the fire?"

"The red fire," corrected the other, "yes, I saw that."

"Did you see me come up to the house?" Minter nodded.

"I even saw you come up to the –" Crash!

They were standing near the window when the interruption came. The big glass pane splintered into a thousand pieces, and something dropped heavily on to the floor. Jerry stared open-mouthed at Minter, as the man stooped and picked up an object from the ground.

"How very cheerful, sir," said Minter holding a large white something in his hand, and despite his self-possession Jeremiah shivered. It was a human skull that had come hurtling through the window!

Jeremiah Jowlett was early in London the following morning, and instead of going to his office, he proceeded straight to Scotland Yard, where he had an interview with the assistant commissioner.

That official listened without comment whilst Jeremiah told his story, and when he had finished:

"What do you want me to do?" he asked.

"I want the best detective you have, sir, preferably Leverett, who I am told is a particularly smart man; for I am sure that behind all these ghostly warnings there is something particularly sinister, and I associate the death of the man Carter –"

"With the ghost?" smiled the commissioner quietly.

"With the ghost," said Jeremiah.

The Commissioner shook his head.

"I am afraid you can't have Leverett; he has been working for some time on a very old case – the Flack case; you probably have heard of it?"

"I know about the Flack gang," smiled Jeremiah, "what is Leverett doing?"

"He has been trying to recover the money that was stolen from the liner. The Flacks got away with an enormous treasure, you will remember, and not a penny of it has been recovered. I can let you have Jackson, who is a fairly smart fellow."

"There is another thing I want to say, Sir John," said Jeremiah, and he seemed reluctant to continue. "It is about my man Minter; a very excellent chap," he explained, "but I have reason to suspect that he knows more of this ghost business – in fact, I am under the impression that he *is* the ghost!"

He took a little case from his inside pocket and produced a photograph.

"I snapped Minter when he wasn't looking the other day; perhaps you people may be able to identify him. I hate thinking ill of the man, who has been a particularly good servant to me, but in the circumstances –"

The commissioner took the photograph from Jerry's hand and examined it.

"Do you know him, sir?"

"I seem to remember the face."

"Is he a member of the Flack gang," said Jerry with sudden inspiration.

"I will ask Leverett," said the commissioner quietly. "And in the meantime Mr Jowlett, I will see that your house is kept under observation. It must be an extremely trying experience for you."

"It will be more trying for the ghost," said Jerry unpleasantly.

He had arranged with Minter to take his clothes and

personal belongings to James Stuart's house, and when he returned that evening it was with a sense of going home.

He found the dutiful Minter very much at his ease in his new surroundings.

"Nothing disturbs that fellow," said Jerry, with reluctant admiration. "You would imagine that he was born and bred in your uncle's service."

Margot laughed.

She was looking unusually beautiful that night, Jerry thought, and he prayed that Mr Stuart's investigations into spiritual phenomena would occupy at least a week, though he felt a little guilty that he had allowed the old man to go up to the house at all. His conscience was pricking him that night at dinner.

"Do you know, Mr Stuart," he blurted out, when they had reached the coffee and dessert stage of the meal, "I think I ought to tell you that these manifestations, as you call them, are due to human agency."

The old man turned his grave eyes upon Jeremiah.

"That is what the uninitiated say of all manifestations," he said quietly.

"But I have a feeling that I am fooling you by allowing you to go to the house," said Jerry.

"I am willing to be fooled," said Stuart with a quiet smile.

"I saw you to-day."

It was the girl who spoke, and she addressed her uncle.

He raised his bristling eyebrows.

"You saw me, my dear," he said gently. "Where did you see me?"

"At Seaford," said the girl with a smile. "You were in a big motor-boat. It was almost too big to call a motor-boat; it was nearly a yacht. I had to go into Seaford to get some medicine for Mrs Wilmot, who has rheumatism," she said.

"You should have gone to Eastbourne, the road isn't so bad," he said shortly and then after a long pause: "Yes, I was trying the boat. A man wishes me to buy it, but I am not very keen on the sea."

"But it was a brand new boat, and they told me it had just arrived from London and that it was yours."

He smiled.

"The wish was probably father to the thought," he said good-humouredly, "and the gentleman who gave you this information was probably the proprietor, who is anxious to sell it to me at a profit."

He changed the conversation to another channel.

At nine o'clock that night, with a small bag in his hand and Jeremiah's keys in his pocket, he said good-night to the two.

"I shall probably have some very important information to give you in the morning," he said. "I am in a particularly good mood to-night, and there is very little doubt that I shall gain communication with those upon the other plane."

"Cheerio," said Jeremiah, who could think of nothing more appropriate to say.

"Poor uncle," said the girl when the older man had gone. "He really does believe in spirits you know."

"I'm inclined to believe in them myself," said Jeremiah flippantly. "In fact, I hope that Down Hill is stiff wth ghosts, then they will keep Mr Stuart busy for another year."

He reached out and took her hand, and saw her colour change.

"Margot," he said, "how long does a man have to know a girl before he falls hopelessly in love with her?"

She tried to withdraw her hand but he held it tightly.

"I know that this is not the most appropriate time for love-making, and that by certain rules of conduct I am acting despicably," he said earnestly, "but Margot, I can answer the question I have just asked. It takes a man just as long as I have known you to fall in love."

"Do you play chess?" she asked hastily.

"I play everything except the flute," said Jeremiah.

He was a riotously happy man that evening, for he had read the answer to his unspoken questions in the moist eyes of the girl, and when he went to bed that night (which was in Mr Stuart's own room) he seemed to tread on air.

The next morning brought James Stuart a little weary-looking, but full of confidence. He had an amazing story to tell of a visitation, and a long conversation he had had with one of the innumerable spirits which haunted Down Hill, but he only stayed for ten minutes and then returned to the house.

Jeremiah went up to town, taking Minter with him. He had a number of purchases to make, and he intended that this Christmas Day should be a memorable one, not only in his own life, but in the life of the woman he loved.

They got back to Arthurton after nightfall, and the snow was falling gently but persistently.

"It looks as if we are going to have a pretty wild night, Minter," said Jerry as he jumped into the car.

"Yes, sir," said Minter agreeably.

The wind was blowing in fitful gusts, and long before they had reached the house, both men were white with the driven flakes.

Jerry could not see Down Hill house: the falling snow made an impenetrable veil which hid, not only the bungalow, but the whole of the hill.

The girl had been busy decorating the house with holly and greenery, and Jerry spent a happy evening assisting her. He allowed Minter, who said he had a chill, to go to bed early, but this was no great hardship to Jerry, who wanted to be alone with the girl, free from interruption.

They had almost finished their work when Jeremiah remembered a particular present which he had given Minter to carry. It was intended for Mr James Stuart and was not amongst the parcels that were piled on the hall table. Minter would not be asleep so early, he thought, and went up the stairs to the room where Minter was quartered. He knocked at the door but there was no answer, and he turned the handle and walked in. The room was empty; the bed had not been slept in, and Jeremiah went back to the girl a very thoughtful young man.

Mrs Wilmot, the housekeeper whose rheumatism had sent the girl into Seaford, had not seen Minter, nor had the other servants who had been employed since Margot's arrival.

"He said he had a chill, and I let him go to bed," said Jeremiah in a troubled voice. "I don't understand it and I don't like it. If he had a chill he would not go out on a night like this, and if he hadn't a chill, he had certainly some reason for lying."

"Perhaps he has gone up to your house for something he had forgotten," suggested Margot. "Now don't be silly, Jeremiah; come along and help me with this holly."

Midnight came and the girl had gone to bed, but still Minter had not returned. Jerry made three visits to his room, and at one o'clock he decided that he would lock up and go to bed. But how would Minter get in? Minter was beginning to worry him. That smooth, placid man, who was never disturbed and never distressed by the most extraordinary happening, was beginning to present a problem almost as insoluble as the Ghost of Down Hill.

At two o'clock Jerry went up to his room and lay down, pulling the silken coverlet over him, expecting any minute to be disturbed by Minter's knock, but no sound came. After lying for an hour he got up and looked out of the window. The snow was still falling, and there was no sound but the low soughing of the wind and the distant hoot of a fog-horn in the far-away Channel.

He wondered what the old man was doing at that lonely house on the hill, and smiled despite his annoyance. Then he heard the low purring of a motor-car. It came to him with the wind in little gusts, sometimes loud, sometimes almost indistinguishible. He threw open the casement windows and leant out, peering into the darkness. Nearer and nearer came the sound of the car, and suddenly with a start he recognized that it was his own car which he had left in the garage on the top of the hill, on the previous night.

There was no mistaking the sound. Jeremiah could have distinguished it from a dozen. Suddenly the purring ceased;

the engine had stopped. Faintly came the sound of a voice; a queer, eerie sound it made in that silent night; high-pitched and unintelligible. Another voice replied, and then there was an interval of silence. Suddenly a shot rang out, clear and distinct. It was followed by another, and a third, in rapid succession.

Jerry waited to hear no more. In three seconds he was outside the house and running through the deep snow in the direction of the road whence the sound had proceeded.

He heard the roar of his car, and jumped aside just in time to avoid being run down; it was going without lights and he only had time to glimpse a huddled figure at the wheel before it passed into the night.

He stood stock still, bewildered and baffled. Then there came to him a faint cry from the direction the car had gone; he plunged through a snow-drift almost up to his waist in an effort to reach the man who had called. Putting his hand in his pocket he discovered his lamp, and flashed the light. He knew before he had picked up his bearings that he was in one of the deep ditches which ran on either side of the road, and he struggled back to firmer going.

"Where are you?" he shouted.

"Here," cried a faint voice, and he turned into the narrow lane which led up to Down Hill farm.

Suddenly he stopped and his blood ran cold. Staring up from the ground was that ghastly fleshless face he had seen on the monk. Only for a second was he stricken motionless, and stooping picked up the thing. It was a mask; evidently dropped by somebody, but was evidently part of the "ghost's" equipment.

"Where are you?" he called again.

"Here," said a voice close at hand, and he turned his lamp on a figure that lay half covered by the driving snowflakes.

"My God," he gasped, "Minter!"

Minter's white face was streaked with blood, but that calm man could afford to smile.

"My name isn't Minter," he smiled. "I am Inspector Leverett of Scotland Yard, and I am afraid I am badly hurt."

It was some time before Jeremiah could procure assistance to carry the wounded man to the house, but at last Leverett was propped up on pillows in the drawing room, and Mrs Wilmot was lighting a fire to prepare restoratives.

Jerry had a rough knowledge of surgery and he saw at once that the two wounds in the man's head and shoulder were not as desperate as he had feared, a view which was confirmed when Arthurton's one doctor came upon the scene.

"Who did this?" asked Jeremiah.

"John Flack," was the reply. "I have been watching him for five months, and now the devil has got away, though he can't escape from England, that I swear. Which way did he go, sir?"

"Was he in the car?" asked Jeremiah.

The man nodded and winced with the pain of it.

"I think he went to Seaford."

"To Seaford," gasped Inspector Leverett. "Didn't I hear the young lady say that he was trying out a motor-boat? That is the means by which John Flack will escape"

"No, it was Mr Stuart who was trying the motor-boat," said Jeremiah.

The man looked round.

"Is the young lady about?" he asked in a low voice.

Jeremiah shook his head.

"No, thank heavens, she's still sleeping, Mrs Wilmot tells me."

"Good," said Leverett, and eyed Jeremiah curiously. "You say that Mr Stuart owned that boat at Seaford," he said, "and I told you that John Flack would escape by means of that boat. I now tell you what will probably surprise you, Mr Jowlett. Flack and James Stuart are one and the same person!"

VIII

Margot Panton never knew the story of her uncle's past. She simply heard that he had gone abroad, and did not even know that wreckage of his motor-boat had been picked up in the Channel four days later. To her James Stuart is still the pleasant memory of a pleasant and eccentric old man who left England hurriedly and unexpectedly on a wild winter night, and has not returned.

Jeremiah saved her from the knowledge, and when he sold his house at Arthurton, and without authority disposed of James Stuart's property, handing the proceeds to the girl, she never dreamt but that he was acting under Mr Stuart's directions.

Even when they married, as they were three months later, Jeremiah never showed her the letter which Inspector Leverett sent to him a week after the girl had been whisked off to town.

"DEAR MR JOWLETT," the letter ran,

"I feel that I owe you an apology and an explanation beyond the few incoherent remarks I made on the night when you undoubtedly saved me from death, for I should have been frozen by the morning.

"You probably know as much about the Flack gang as I do. The gang was organized by one of the cleverest crooks in the world; his real name was James Stuart. Stuart had been in the hands of the police many times, but always under the name of John Flack. He was a clever bank smasher and for his crimes he served three terms of penal servitude. His long absences from home, when he was supposed to be engaged in tours of Brazil and South America generally, are explained by the fact that he was serving terms of penal servitude during these periods.

"Nobody knew that the white-bearded gentleman who lived at Arthurton was Flack, and I had no suspicion of the circumstances until some six months ago. Flack, or Stuart's last job, was the burgling of the strong room of a liner. He and his two companions got away with nearly a million dollars in paper currency, with the police hot on their track. The third man of the gang was drowned in an attempt to swim a river, but Flack and the man named Sibby Carter went their several ways, agreeing to meet in London at a certain rendezvous. The police picked up Sibby Carter, and from him learnt the direction Flack had taken, and started off in pursuit of the leader of the gang. Flack or Stuart, must have known what was happening, for he made a bee-line to the country he knew best, namely the country about Arthurton where he lived, respected by his neighbours, who had not the slightest idea that they were harbouring one of the greatest crooks in the world.

"He dare not go home, however. His biggest asset was his identity as Stuart, and he had a shrewd suspicion that the police would not be shaken off. He arrived at Arthurton in the night, and his first step was to bury his plunder. He chose a spot on the top of a hill, the site of an old monastery which was supposed to be haunted. There, deep in the ground, he buried a steel box containing his loot.

"After carefully marking the place, he went on to London, hoping to baffle his pursuers, but was arrested at Charing Cross station, two days later. He swore that the money was lost, and was sent to a term of penal servitude for seven years, as also was his confederate, Carter. The two men were released within a few days of one another, but unfortunately Flack was released first. Carter, who wanted his share of the loot, and who knew that his chief had hidden it, began a search to discover the hiding place of his former leader.

"He must have known something about Stuart's identity, for the man appeared in Arthurton a short time after his release. It was his arrival at Arthurton which brought me, for I was trailing Sibby Carter in the hopes that it would bring me to the stolen property which had been hidden. Carter was anxious to get the money, but he was also in some fear of Stuart, for I have no evidence that he had ever spoken to the man, except on that night when he lost his life. But here I anticipate.

"Stuart, released from gaol, came back home and discovered to his horror that a bungalow had been erected on the very spot where his money was hidden. His first suspicion was that the builder, or the Clerk of the Works must have found the money and said nothing about it. He paid a visit to the Clerk of the Works, who by this time had an appointment with the municipality of Eastbourne, and holding the man up at the point of a pistol, he examined his pass-books, his object being to discover whether any large sum had been paid into the account at the time the building was in course of erection. Failing to make this discovery he next called upon the builder, a man named Staines, and submitted him to the same search. When these had failed, he was certain that the money was still under the house, and began his carefully considered plan of frightening the occupant away so that he could pursue his search without hindrance.

"Unfortunately for him, I had already arrived at Arthurton and knowing that Sibby Carter was in the neighbourhood, and more than suspecting that James Stuart and Flack were one and the same person, I had contrived to be taken into your employment as a butler – in which capacity I trust I have given you no cause for complaint.

"I shaved off my beard and moustache, and it was fortunate for me that I did so, otherwise Stuart would have recognized me.

"On the night that Sibby Carter was killed I was watching the house with a pair of powerful night glasses, and I saw the two men in conversation. They must have walked to the porch, and there undoubtedly James Stuart, who was a tremendously powerful old man, had broken the neck of his erstwhile companion in crime, in order to silence him. Possibly Carter had threatened to expose Stuart. The motive for the murder is not at all obscure; there were many reasons why it was necessary that Carter should be put out of the way.

"The rest of the story needs no telling. Stuart, posing as a spiritualist, got admission to your house. On the night he dug deep into your cellar and unearthed the tin box, I was watching him. I followed him down the hill road through the storm, hanging on to the back of the car, knowing that he was making his final getaway, and that the tin box on the seat by his side contained the money he had stolen from the liner.

"When we reached the road I thought it was time to reveal myself, and jumping on to the step, I put a revolver under his nose and demanded his surrender. At the same time I gripped the steel box and jerked it from the car. Before I knew what had happened, he had shot me down – that is the story.

"The money is now recovered, and I should not think it is necessary that Miss Panton should know any more than she already knows.

"One thing I think you can tell her – it is that her uncle, definitely and finally, has laid the Ghost of Down Hill.

"Yours very sincerely,
FREDERICK LEVERETT."